WeeSing

AMERICA

by
Pamela Conn Beall and
Susan Hagen Nipp

Illustrated by
Nancy Spence Klein

PRICE STERN SLOAN
Los Angeles

To our patriots and pioneers —
past, present and future

With special thanks to our Wee Singers: Ryan and Devin Nipp;
Hilary, Sean, Kyle and Lindsay Beall; Sam, Erin and Katie Klein;
Rachel, Peter and John Macy...

And to our musical producers,
Barry Hagen and Mauri Macy

Printed on recycled paper

Cover Illustration by Dennis Hockerman

Copyright © 1987 by Pamela Conn Beall and Susan Hagen Nipp
Published by Price Stern Sloan, Inc.
A member of The Putnam & Grosset Group, New York, New York.

ISBN: 0-8431-3805-X

15 14 13 12

PREFACE

Singing "The Star Spangled Banner" before a baseball game, watching fireworks on the 4th of July, seeing the Statue of Liberty with her arm raised high — what feelings these evoke. There seems to be an American spirit in all of us; a pride in our people, our land, our freedom.

Wee Sing America is a tribute to this nation and to all the generations that have created it. We have collected songs about our land and our flag, about war and peace and about the people who explored, settled and built our country. These are all songs that were created and sung by our forefathers. When we sing them, we seem to feel a little closer to our history and have a greater understanding of our heritage.

As we researched innumerable sources, we were stirred by the events which led to the creation of the songs. We have included many of these facts to add to your understanding of the music.

"We the people of the United States" includes all of us. We are a diverse group, but one nation, one family. We hope through the singing of the songs in this book, you will feel a sense of pride and reflect on what our country was, what it is now and what it will become.

Pam Beall
Susan Nipp

TABLE OF CONTENTS

A PROUD NATION

A GROWING NATION

A Proud Nation

Facts About the USA

Flag:

1775-1777	1777-1794	1959-present

Form of Government: Republic (Democracy)
A government in which the people hold the ruling power through elected representatives

Capital: Washington, D.C.
Site chosen by George Washington in 1791

Motto: In God We Trust
Adopted July 30, 1956

National Anthem: "The Star Spangled Banner"
Adopted March 3, 1931

Bird: Bald Eagle
Adopted June 20, 1782

Flower: Rose
Adopted Oct. 7, 1986

Highest Elevation: Mt. McKinley in Alaska
20,320 feet above sea level

Lowest Elevation: Death Valley in California
282 feet below sea level

Longest River: Mississippi
2,348 miles

Sousa was a famous composer of marches and was the conductor of the United States Marine Band.

WE LOVE THE U.S.A.
(Tune: El Capitán)

B.P. Krone, 1956   John Philip Sousa, 1896

1. We love the U. S. A., We live in a land where men are free And proud to defend their lib-er-ty, We mean it when we say, "We're glad we're a-live and live in the U. S. A." —

2. We love the USA,
    We'll join in the chorus loud and strong,
And sing of the land where we belong.
    We mean it when we say, —
"We're glad we're alive and live in the USA."

*Optional chords for guitar: Key of E (A, B[7], E)

John F. Kennedy

Ask not what your country can do for you, but what you can do for your country.

Inaugural Address, January 20, 1961

The words to "The Star-Spangled Banner" were written by Key during the War of 1812. He had watched the bombing of Fort McHenry by the British and at dawn saw the American flag still flying. He knew the British attack had been turned back.

THE STAR SPANGLED BANNER

Francis Scott Key, 1814   *John Stafford Smith, 1700's*

Oh,— say, can you see, by the dawn's ear-ly light,

What so proud-ly we hailed at the twi-light's last

gleam-ing, Whose broad stripes and bright stars,

through the per-i-lous fight, O'er the ram-parts we

watched were so gal-lant-ly stream-ing? And the
rock-et's red glare, the bombs burst-ing in air, Gave
proof through the night that our flag was still
there. Oh, say, does that — Star Span-gled
Ban-ner — yet — wave, — O'er the land — of the
free and the home of the brave?

★ ★

Preamble to the Constitution
(1787)

We the people of the United States, in order to form a more perfect
Union, establish justice, insure domestic tranquility, provide for the
common defense, promote the general welfare, and secure the blessings
of liberty to ourselves and our posterity, do ordain and establish this
Constitution for the United States of America.

★ ★

YOU'RE A GRAND OLD FLAG

G.M.C.

George M. Cohan, 1905

You're a grand old flag, you're a high fly-ing flag;

And for-ev-er in peace, may you wave;—You're the

em-blem of the land I love, The home of the

free and the brave.— Ev-'ry heart beats true

'neath the Red, White and Blue, Where there's nev-

er a boast or brag;—But, should auld ac-quaint-ance

be for-got, Keep your eye on the grand old flag.—

Cohan was an American actor, playwright, theatrical producer and writer of popular songs.

Pledge to the Flag

I pledge allegiance to the flag of the United States of America and to the Republic for which it stands, one Nation under God, indivisible, with liberty and justice for all.

Written by Francis Bellamy in 1892 to celebrate the 400th anniversary of the discovery of America.

THREE CHEERS FOR THE RED, WHITE AND BLUE
(From the song, "Columbia, the Gem of the Ocean")

Three — cheers for the Red, White and Blue,

Three — cheers for the Red, White and Blue!

The — flag of A-mer-i-ca for-ev-er,

Three — cheers—for the Red, White and Blue!

THE STARS AND STRIPES FOREVER

J.P.S.

John Philip Sousa, 1897

Hur-rah for the flag of the free,— May it
wave as our stan-dard for-ev-er, The gem of the
land and the sea,— The — ban-ner of the
right.— Let des-pots* re-mem-ber the day —
When our fa-thers with might— y en-deav-or, Pro-
claimed as they marched to the fray;** That by their
might, and by their right, It waves for-ev-er!

* despot - absolute ruler
** fray - battle

THERE ARE MANY FLAGS

M.H. Howliston   *Traditional*

1. There are man-y flags in man-y lands, There are flags of ev-'ry hue. But there is no flag how-ev-er grand, Like our own Red, White-and-Blue.

Chorus

Then hur-rah for the flag, our coun-try's flag, Its stripes and white stars, too. There — is no flag in an-y land Like our own Red, White—and—Blue.

2. We shall always love the stars and stripes,
   And we ever shall be true
To this land of ours and the dear old flag,
   Our own Red, White and Blue.
   Chorus

AMERICA

Samuel Francis Smith, 1832

Unknown, 1500's

1. My coun-try,'tis of thee, Sweet land of lib-er-ty, Of thee I sing. Land where my fa-thers died, Land of the Pil-grims'pride, From ev—'ry—moun-tain-side Let—free-dom ring!

2. My native country, thee,
     Land of the noble free,
   Thy name I love.
     I love thy rocks and rills,
   Thy woods and templed hills;
     My heart with rapture thrills
   Like that above.

3. Our fathers' God, to Thee,
     Author of liberty,
   To thee we sing,
     Long may our land be bright
   With freedom's holy light;
     Protect us by Thy might,
   Great God, our King!

The tune of "America" has been known for over two centuries in many European countries, the most familiar being the British national anthem.

14

Thomas Jefferson

We hold these truths to be self-evident: that all men are created equal, that they are endowed by their Creator with certain inalienable rights, that among these are life, liberty, and the pursuit of happiness.

from The Declaration of Independence, 1776

Abraham Lincoln

Four score and seven years ago our fathers brought forth on this continent a new nation, conceived in liberty, and dedicated to the proposition that all men are created equal.

from The Gettysburg Address, 1863

Martin Luther King

I have a dream that one day this nation will rise up and live out the true meaning of its creed: "We hold these truths to be self-evident: that all men are created equal."

Washington, D.C., March, 1963

AMERICA, AMERICA
(Round)

S.N. & P.B. 1609

A - mer-i-ca, A - mer-i-ca, Land of hope and lib-er—ty, Free-dom rings from ev-'ry—moun-tain, From sea to sea.—

15

The magnificent view from Pike's Peak in Colorado inspired Bates, an English teacher, to write this poem. The melody was originally a hymn.

AMERICA THE BEAUTIFUL

Katharine Lee Bates, 1893   Samuel A. Ward, 1882

1. O beau-ti-ful for spa-cious skies, For am-ber waves of grain, For pur-ple moun-tain maj-es-ties A-bove the fruit-ed plain! A-mer-i-ca! A-mer-i-ca! God shed His grace on thee, And crown thy good with broth-er-hood From sea to shin-ing sea!

2. O beautiful for pilgrim feet
     Whose stern, impassioned stress
   A thoroughfare for freedom beat
     Across the wilderness!
   America! America!
     God mend thine every flaw,
   Confirm thy soul in self-control,
     Thy liberty in law!
3. O beautiful for heroes proved
     In liberating strife,
   Who more than self their country loved,
     And mercy more than life!
   America! America!
     May God thy gold refine
   Till all success be nobleness
     And every gain divine!
4. O beautiful for patriot dream
     That sees beyond the years
   Thine alabaster cities gleam
     Undimmed by human tears!
   America! America!
     God shed his grace on thee
   And crown thy good with brotherhood
     From sea to shining sea!

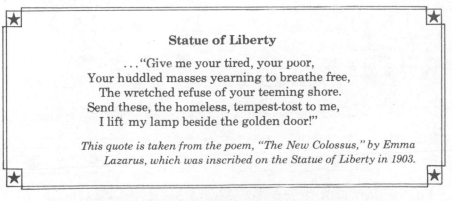

Statue of Liberty

... "Give me your tired, your poor,
Your huddled masses yearning to breathe free,
The wretched refuse of your teeming shore.
Send these, the homeless, tempest-tost to me,
I lift my lamp beside the golden door!"

This quote is taken from the poem, "The New Colossus," by Emma Lazarus, which was inscribed on the Statue of Liberty in 1903.

THE UNITED STATES

S.N.

Susan Nipp

The U-ni-ted States, the U-ni-ted States, I love my coun-try, the U-ni-ted States. There's Al-a-bam-a, A-las-ka, Ar-i-zo-na, Ar-kan-sas, Cal-i-for-nia, Col-o-ra-do, Con-nect-i-cut and Del-a-ware, Flor-i-da, Geor-gia, Ha-wai-i and I-da-ho, Il-li-nois, In-di-an-a, I-o-wa and Kan-sas. Ken-tuck-y, Lou-i-si-an-a, Maine, Mar-y-land, Mas-sa-chu-setts, Mich-i-gan, Min-ne-so-ta, Mis-sis-sip-pi, Mis-sour-i,

18

Mon-tan-a, Ne-bras-ka, Ne-vad-a, New Hamp-shire, New
Jer-sey, New Mex-i-co, New York, North 'n' South Car-o-li-na,
North Da-ko-ta, South Da-ko-ta, O-hi-o, O-kla-hom';
Or-e-gon, Penn-syl-va-nia, Rhode Is-land, Ten-nes-see,
Tex-as, U-tah, Ver-mont, Vir-gin — ia,
West Vir-gin-ia, Wash-ing-ton, Wis-con-sin, Wy-o-ming,
The U-ni-ted States, the U-ni-ted States, I
love my coun-try, the U-nit-ed States. (yeah)
(whisper)

Presidents of the United States

1. George Washington .... 1789 - 1797
2. John Adams... 1797 - 1801
3. Thomas Jefferson .... 1801 - 1809
4. James Madison .... 1809 - 1817
5. James Monroe .... 1817 - 1825
6. John Quincy Adams .... 1825 - 1829
7. Andrew Jackson .... 1829 - 1837
8. Martin Van Buren .... 1837 - 1841
9. William H. Harrison 1841
10. John Tyler .... 1841 - 1845
11. James K. Polk.. 1845 - 1849
12. Zachary Taylor....................................... 1849 - 1850
13. Millard Fillmore .... 1850 - 1853
14. Franklin Pierce .... 1853 - 1857
15. James Buchanan...................................... 1857 - 1861
16. Abraham Lincoln .... 1861 - 1865
17. Andrew Johnson .... 1865 - 1869
18. Ulysses S. Grant..................................... 1869 - 1877
19. Rutherford B. Hayes .... 1877 - 1881
20. James A. Garfield.................................... 1881
21. Chester A. Arthur.................................... 1881 - 1885
22. Grover Cleveland .... 1885 - 1889
23. Benjamin Harrison .... 1889 - 1893
24. Grover Cleveland .... 1893 - 1897
25. William McKinley..................................... 1897 - 1901
26. Theodore Roosevelt .... 1901 - 1909
27. William H. Taft .... 1909 - 1913
28. Woodrow Wilson .... 1913 - 1921
29. Warren G. Harding .... 1921 - 1923
30. Calvin Coolidge .... 1923 - 1929
31. Herbert C. Hoover .... 1929 - 1933
32. Franklin D. Roosevelt................................ 1933 - 1945
33. Harry S. Truman .... 1945 - 1953
34. Dwight D. Eisenhower .... 1953 - 1961
35. John F. Kennedy...................................... 1961 - 1963
36. Lyndon B. Johnson .... 1963 - 1969
37. Richard M. Nixon .... 1969 - 1974
38. Gerald R. Ford....................................... 1974 - 1977
39. Jimmy Carter... 1977 - 1981
40. Ronald Reagan.. 1981 - 1989
41. George Bush .... 1989 - 1993
42. William Clinton....................................... 1993 -

YANKEE DOODLE BOY

G.M.C.

George M. Cohan, 1904

I'm a yan-kee Doo-dle Dan-dy, A yan-kee

Doo-dle do or die;— A real live neph-ew of my

Un - cle Sam, Born on the Fourth of Ju-

ly.— I've got a yan-kee Doo-dle sweet-

heart, She's my Yan - kee Doo-dle joy.—

yan-kee Doo-dle came to Lon-don, just to ride the

po-nies, I am a Yan-kee Doo-dle Boy.—

"Yankee Doodle" was originally sung by the British soldiers to poke fun at the poorly dressed and awkward colonial soldiers during the French and Indian War (1754-1763). Later, during the Revolutionary War (1775-1783), the song became popular with the colonists and they adopted it as their own.

YANKEE DOODLE

Richard Shuckburgh, 1755

European, 1600's

1. Yan-kee Doo-dle went to town a-rid-ing on a po-ny;
Stuck a feath-er in his cap and called it mac-a-ro-ni.

Chorus
Yank-ee Doo-dle, keep it up, Yank-ee Doo-dle dan-dy,
Mind the mu-sic and the step, and with the girls be han-dy.

2. Father and I went down to camp
    Along with Captain Gooding,
And there we saw the men and boys
    As thick as hasty pudding.
        Chorus
3. There was Captain Washington
    Upon a slapping stallion,
A-giving orders to his men,
    I guess there was a million.
        Chorus

OLD ABE LINCOLN

1. Old Abe Lin-coln came—out of the wil-der-ness, Out of the wil-der-ness, Out of the wil-der-ness, Old Abe Lin-coln came—out of the wil-der-ness, Down in Il-li-nois.

2. Old Abe Lincoln was our sixteenth President,
   Sixteenth President, sixteenth President,
   Old Abe Lincoln was our sixteenth President,
   Many long years ago.
3. Old Abe Lincoln freed our nation from slavery,
   Nation from slavery, nation from slavery,
   Old Abe Lincoln freed our nation from slavery,
   Many long years ago.

Abraham Lincoln

...this nation, under God, shall have a new birth of freedom; the government of the people, by the people and for the people, shall not perish from the earth.

from The Gettysburg Address, 1863

23

This song was originally written for a minstrel show. It became popular with the Confederate army during the Civil War.

DIXIE

D.D.E.

Daniel D. Emmett, 1859

I — wish I was — in the land of cot-ton,

Old times there are not for-got-ten, Look a-

way! Look a-way! Look a-way! Dix-ie Land.

In — Dix-ie Land — where — I was born in,

Ear-ly on one frost-y morn-in; Look a-way!

Look a-way! Look a-way! Dix-ie Land.

24

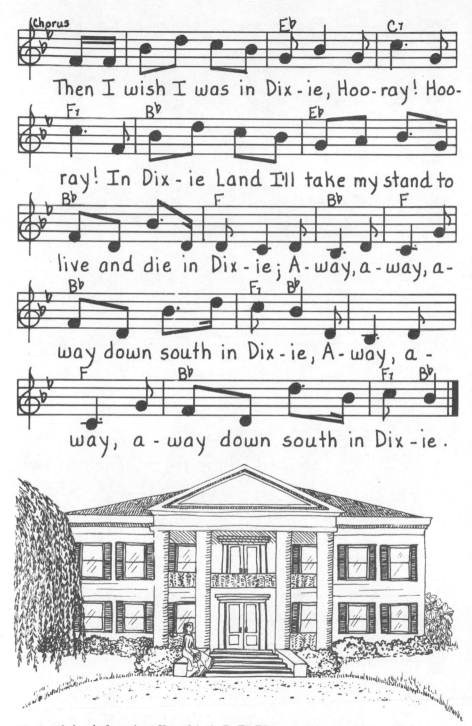

(Chorus)

Then I wish I was in Dix-ie, Hoo-ray! Hoo-ray! In Dix-ie Land I'll take my stand to live and die in Dix-ie; A-way, a-way, a-way down south in Dix-ie, A-way, a-way, a-way down south in Dix-ie.

*Optional chords for guitar: Key of A (A, D, E⁷, B⁷)

During the Civil War, Howe heard the Union soldiers singing "John Brown's Body." The melody stayed with her and during the night she arose from bed and wrote the words of the Battle Hymn.

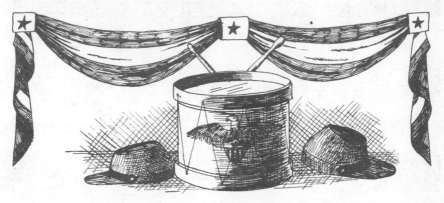

BATTLE HYMN OF THE REPUBLIC

Julia Ward Howe, 1861   *Unknown*

1. Mine eyes have seen the glo-ry of the com-ing of the Lord; He is tramp-ling out the vin-tage where the grapes of wrath are stored; He hath loos'd the fate-ful light-ning of His ter-ri-ble swift sword, His truth is march-ing on.

26

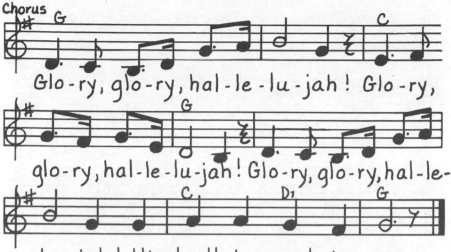

Chorus

Glo-ry, glo-ry, hal-le-lu-jah! Glo-ry, glo-ry, hal-le-lu-jah! Glo-ry, glo-ry, hal-le-lu-jah! His truth is march-ing on.

2. I have seen Him in the watch-fires of a hundred circling camps;
   They have builded Him an altar in the evening dews and damps;
   I can read His righteous sentence by the dim and flaring lamps,
   His day is marching on.
      Chorus

3. He has sounded forth the trumpet that shall never call retreat;
   He is sifting out the hearts of men before His judgment seat.
   Oh, be swift, my soul, to answer Him! Be jubilant, my feet!
   Our God is marching on.
      Chorus

4. In the beauty of the lilies Christ was born across the sea,
   With a glory in His bosom that transfigures you and me;
   As He died to make men holy let us die to make men free,
   While God is marching on.
      Chorus

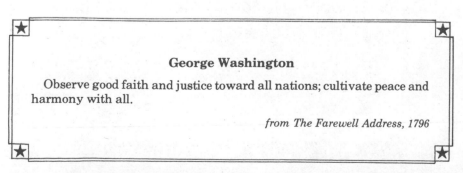

George Washington

Observe good faith and justice toward all nations; cultivate peace and harmony with all.

from The Farewell Address, 1796

WHEN JOHNNY COMES MARCHING HOME

Patrick S. Gilmore, 1863   *Irish Folk Tune*

1. When John-ny comes march-ing home a-gain, Hur-rah! Hur-rah! We'll give him a heart-y wel-come then, Hur-rah! Hur-rah! The— men will cheer, — the boys will shout, The la-dies they— will all turn out, And we'll all feel gay when John-ny comes march-ing home!—

The official bandmaster of the Union Army, Patrick Gilmore (pseud. Louis Lambert), wrote the words to this song during the Civil War.

2. The old church bell will peal with joy,
   Hurrah! Hurrah!
   To welcome home our darling boy,
   Hurrah! Hurrah!
   The village lads and lassies say
   With roses they will strew the way,
   And we'll all feel gay
   When Johnny comes marching home!
3. Get ready for the jubilee,
   Hurrah! Hurrah!
   We'll give the heroes three times three,
   Hurrah! Hurrah!
   The laurel wreath is ready now
   To place upon his loyal brow,
   And we'll all feel gay
   When Johnny comes marching home!
4. Let love and friendship on that day,
   Hurrah! Hurrah!
   Their choicest treasures then display,
   Hurrah! Hurrah!
   And let each one perform some part,
   To fill with joy the warrior's heart,
   And we'll all feel gay
   When Johnny comes marching home!

GOOBER PEAS

Civil War Song, 1864

1. Sit-ting by the road-side on a sum-mer's day,

Chat-ting with my mess-mates, pas-sing time a-way,

Ly-ing in the sha-dow—un-der-neath the trees,

Good-ness, how de-li-cious,— eat-ing goo-ber peas.

Chorus

Peas, peas, peas, peas, eat-ing goo-ber peas,

Good-ness, how de-li-cious,— eat-ing goo-ber peas.

2. When a horseman passes, the soldiers have a rule,
   To cry out at their loudest, "Mister, get a mule."
   But still another pleasure, enchanting more than these,
   Is wearing out your grinders, eating goober peas.
   Chorus

3. Just before the battle, the general hears a row,
   He says, "The Yanks are coming. I hear their rifles now."
   He turns around in wonder, and what d'you think he sees?
   The Georgia militia, eating goober peas.
   Chorus

*During the last days of the Civil War, the Confederate soldiers were short on rations, so they
ate goober peas (peanuts).*

THE CAISSONS

E.L.G.

Edmund L. Gruber, 1908

O-ver hill, o-ver dale, we have hit the dust-y trail,

And those cais-sons go rol-ling a-long.— In and out,

hear them shout, "Coun-ter-march and right a-bout,"

And those cais-sons go rol-ling a-long.— Then it's

Hi! Hi! Hee! In the Field Ar-til-ler-y, Sound off your

num-bers loud and strong,— Wher-e'er you go, you will

al-ways know That those cais-sons are rol-ling a-long,

"Keep 'em rol-ling!" And those cais-sons go rol-ling a-long.—
(shout)

MARINE'S HYMN

Unknown Marine, 1847   *French Tune*

From the halls of Mon-te-zu—ma, To the

shores of Tri-po-li, We—fight our coun-try's

bat—tles, In the air, on land, and sea. First to

fight for right and free—dom, And to keep our

hon-or clean; We are proud to claim the

ti—tle of U-nit-ed States Ma-rines.

ANCHORS AWEIGH

Alfred H. Miles

Charles A. Zimmerman, 1907

An-chors a-weigh, my boys, An-chors a-weigh, Fare-

well to col-lege joys, We sail at break of day,—— Stand

Na-vy out to sea, Through swirl-ing foam, Un-til we

meet once more, Here's wish-ing you a hap-py voy-age home.

A Growing Nation

SWEET BETSY FROM PIKE

Pioneer Song, 1849

1. Did you ev-er hear of sweet Bet-sy from Pike,

Who crossed the wide prai-ries with her hus-band, Ike,

With two yoke of cat-tle and one spot-ted hog, A—

tall Shang-hai roos-ter and an old yel-ler dog?

Chorus

Sing—too-ral-i, oo-ral-i, oo-ral-i ay,

Sing—too-ral-i, oo-ral-i, oo-ral-i ay.

2. The alkali* desert was burning and bare,
   And Ike cried in fear, "We are lost, I declare!
   My dear old Pike County, I'll go back to you."
   Said Betsy, "You'll go by yourself, if you do."
   Chorus

3. They swam the wide rivers and crossed the tall peaks,
   They camped on the prairie for weeks upon weeks,
   They fought off the Indians with musket and ball,
   And reached California in spite of it all.
   Chorus

* mineral salt

35

I'VE BEEN WORKIN' ON THE RAILROAD

Railroad Work Song

I've been work-in' on the rail-road, All the live-long day,

I've been work-in' on the rail-road, Just to pass the time a-

way, Don't you hear the whis-tle blow-in', Rise up so ear-ly in the

morn; Don't you hear the cap-tain shout-ing, "Di-nah, blow your

horn!" Di-nah, won't you blow, Di-nah, won't you blow,

Di-nah, won't you blow your horn,— Di-nah, won't you blow,

Di-nah, won't you blow, Di-nah, won't you blow your horn!

Some-one's in the Kit-chen with Di-nah, Some-one's in the

Kit-chen, I Know,——Some-one's in the Kit-chen with Di-nah,

Strum-min' on the old ban-jo And sing-in', Fee, Fi,

Fid-dlee-i-o, Fee, Fi, Fid-dlee-i-o,—— Fee, Fi,

Fid-dlee-i-o, Strum-min' on the old ban-jo.

The year 1830 marked the beginning of the railroad era in the US. The Gold Rush in 1849 speeded its development and in 1869 the rails stretched from the Atlantic to the Pacific when the Union Pacific and Central Pacific Railroads were joined at Promontory, Utah.

John Henry was a black railroad worker who apparently died around 1873 during the construction of the Big Bend Tunnel in West Virginia on the C & O railroad.

JOHN HENRY

Railroad Ballad

1. When John Hen-ry was a lit-tle ba-by,—
Sit-tin' on his dad-dy's knee, He picked up a
ham-mer and a lit-tle piece of steel, said, "This
ham-mer's gon-na be the death of me, Lawd, Lawd,
This ham-mer's gon-na be the death of me."

2. Well, the Captain said to John Henry,
    "Gonna bring that steam drill 'round.
Gonna bring that steam drill out on the job,
    Gonna whop that steel on down, Lawd, Lawd,
Gonna whop that steel on down."

3. John Henry told his captain,
    Said, "A man ain't nothin' but a man,
But before I'd let that steam drill beat me down,
    I'd die with this hammer in my hand, Lawd, Lawd,
I'd die with this hammer in my hand."

4. Well, the man that invented the steam drill,
    He thought he was mighty fine,
  But John Henry drove his fifteen feet,
    And the steam drill only made nine, Lawd, Lawd,
  The stream drill only made nine.
5. John Henry was hammerin' on the mountain,
    And his hammer was strikin' fire,
  He drove so hard that he broke his poor old heart,
    And he laid down his hammer and he died, Lawd, Lawd,
  He laid down his hammer and he died.
6. They took John Henry to the graveyard,
    And they buried him in the sand,
  And ev'ry locomotive that comes roarin' by
    Says, "There lies a steel drivin' man," Lawd, Lawd,
  "There lies a steel drivin' man."

The Irishmen who worked on the railroads were called "tarriers." Two explanations for this name have been passed down: One, that their red, stubby beards made them look like terrier dogs; or two, that they did not tarry (move slowly) as they worked.

DRILL, YE TARRIERS

T.C.

Thomas Casey, 1888

1. Ev-'ry morn-ing at sev-en o'clock, There's twen-ty tar-ri-ers a-work-in' on the rock, And the boss comes a-long and he says, "Keep still, And come down heav-y on the cast i-ron drill."

*Optional chords for guitar: Key of Am (Am, E⁷, G)

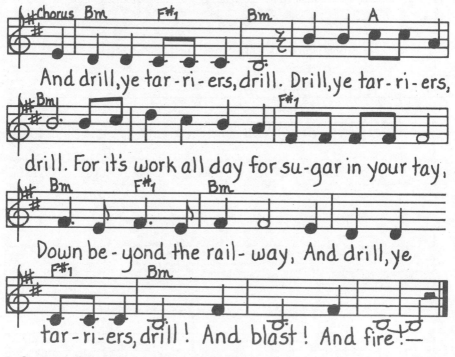

And drill, ye tar-ri-ers, drill. Drill, ye tar-ri-ers, drill. For it's work all day for su-gar in your tay, Down be-yond the rail-way, And drill, ye tar-ri-ers, drill! And blast! And fire!—

2. Our new foreman was Dan McCann,
   By gosh, he was a blame mean man;
   Last week a premature blast went off,
   And a mile in the air went big Jim Goff.
       Chorus
3. Next time pay day comes around,
   Jim Goff a dollar short was found;
   "What for?" says he, then this reply,
   "You're docked for the time you were up in the sky."
       Chorus

41

During the Irish potato famine of 1840, thousands of Irishmen came to America. Many found jobs working on the railroads.

PADDY WORKS ON THE RAILWAY

Railroad Ballad

1. In eight-een hun-dred and for-ty one, I put me cor-du-roy breech-es on, I put me cor-du-roy breech-es on To work up-on the rail-way.

Chorus

Fil-i-me-oo-ree-eye-ree-ay, Fil-i-me-oo-ree-eye-ree-ay, Fil-i-me-oo-ree-eye-ree-ay, To work up-on the rail-way.

2. It's "Pat, do this" and "Pat, do that," without a stocking or cravat*,
   And nothing but an old straw hat, while Pat works on the railway.
   Chorus
3. And, when Pat lays him down to sleep, the wiry bugs around him creep,
   And hardly a bit can poor Pat sleep, while he works on the railway.
   Chorus

* necktie or scarf

After the Civil War, cattle raising became an important industry. Cowboys trailed herds to railroad towns where dealers shipped the cattle to Chicago and other meat-packing centers. The Chisholm Trail, which ran from the Mexican border through Texas to Abilene, Kansas, was often used.

THE OLD CHISHOLM TRAIL

Cowboy Song

1. Oh, come a-long boys and lis-ten to my tale, I'll— tell you of my trou-bles on the old Chis-holm Trail,

(chorus) Sing-in' Ki-yi yip-pi yip-pi yay, yip-pi yay! Sing-in' Ki-yi yip-pi yip-pi yay.—

2. I started on the trail on June twenty-third,
    With a drove of Texas cattle, 2000 in the herd,
        Chorus

3. I'm up in the mornin' before daylight,
    And before I sleep, the moon shines bright,
        Chorus

4. Oh, it's bacon and beans 'most every day,
    I'd as soon be a-eatin' prairie hay,
        Chorus

5. My feet are in the stirrups and my rope is on the side,
    Show me a hoss that I can't ride,
        Chorus

* Optional chords for guitar: Key of E (E, B⁷)

43

GOOD-BYE, OLD PAINT

Cowboy Song

1. My foot in the stir-rup, my po-ny won't stand,—
   I'm a-leav-in' Chey-enne, I'm off for Mon-tan;—

Chorus

Good-bye, old Paint, I'm a-leav-in' Chey-enne,

Good-bye, old Paint, I'm a-leav-in' Chey-enne.

2. I'm a-ridin' old Paint, I'm a-leadin' old Dam,
   Good-bye, little Annie, I'm off for Montan'.
   Chorus
3. Oh, hitch up your horses and feed 'em some hay,
   And seat yourself by me as long as you stay.
   Chorus
4. My horses ain't hungry, they'll not eat your hay,
   My wagon is loaded and rolling away.
   Chorus

Optional accomp: Play only D chord throughout.

44

I RIDE AN OLD PAINT

Cowboy Song

I ride an old paint,*—I lead an old dam,*—I'm goin' to Mon-tan-a to throw the hoo-li-han.* They feed in the cou-lees,* they wa-ter in the draw,* Their tails are all mat-ted, their backs are all raw.

Ride a-round, lit-tle do-gies,* Ride a-round—them— slow, For the fi-'ry* and snuf-fy* are rar-in' to go.

* Definitions:
paint - spotted horse
dam - mother of a foal
throw the hoolihan - to rope a steer and wrestle to the ground
coulees - ravines
draw - a ravine which drains water after a hard rain
dogies - motherless calves
fiery - spirited
snuffy - disagreeable

Cattle that weren't driven to railroad towns were often trailed to stock ranges in northern states such as Wyoming, Montana and the Dakotas. These ranges were left open to grazing when buffalo herds were destroyed.

GIT ALONG, LITTLE DOGIES*

Cowboy Song, 1860's

1. As I was a-walk-ing one morn-ing for
pleas-ure, I spied a cow punch-er a-
rid-ing a-long. His hat was throwed
back and his spurs was a-jing-ling, And
as he ap-proached, he was sing-ing this song:

* motherless calves

46

Whoop-ee ti - yi -yo, git a-long lit-tle do-gies, It's your mis-for-tune and none of my own. Whoop-ee ti-yi-yo, git a-long lit-tle do-gies, For you know Wy-o-ming will be your new home.

2. It's early in spring that we round up the dogies,
   We mark 'em and brand 'em and bob off their tails,
   We round up the horses, load up the chuck wagon,
   And then throw the dogies out on the long trail.
       Chorus
3. Some fellows go up the trail for pleasure,
   But that's where they get it most awfully wrong,
   For you haven't an idea the trouble they give us,
   As we go driving those dogies along.
       Chorus

47

MY HOME'S IN MONTANA

Cowboy Song

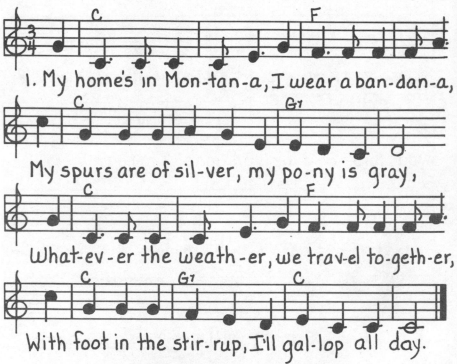

1. My home's in Mon-tan-a, I wear a ban-dan-a,

My spurs are of sil-ver, my po-ny is gray,

What-ev-er the weath-er, we trav-el to-geth-er,

With foot in the stir-rup, I'll gal-lop all day.

2. We're up with the sun, there's work to be done,
   In the wide open spaces, that's where we would be,
Out here in the West is the life we love best,
   Montana is home for my pony and me.
3. When far from the ranches, I chop the pine branches
   To heap on the campfire as daylight grows pale,
When I have partaken of beans and of bacon,
   I whistle a cheery old song of the trail.

The lives of the roving cowboys changed when the government opened the land to farmers and ranchers who staked out their homesteads and fenced their property.

OLD TEXAS

Cowboy Song

1. I'm goin' to leave (I'm goin' to leave) ol'—Tex-as now, (ol'—Tex-as now,) They've got no use (They've got no use) for the long-horned cow. (for the long-horned cow.)

Descant (optional)

clip, clop, clip, clop,

2. They've plowed and fenced my cattle range,
   And the people there are all so strange.
3. I'll take my horse, I'll take my rope,
   And hit the trail upon a lope*.
4. I'll bid adios to the Alamo,
   And set my face toward Mexico.
5. I'll spend my days on the wide, wide range,
   For the people there are not so strange.
6. The hard, hard ground will be my bed,
   And the saddle seat will hold my head.
7. And when I waken from my dreams,
   I'll eat my bread and my sardines.

* gallop

In the 1890s, a tiny black bug from Mexico called a boll weevil invaded the Texas cotton fields by the millions. Nothing could stop them and they multiplied quickly. Great destruction of crops occurred and poverty followed.

THE BOLL WEEVIL

Southern Ballad

1. The boll wee-vil is a— lit-tle black bug,

Come from Mex-i-co they say, Come all the way to—

Tex-as, Just a-look-in' for a place to stay,

Just a-look-in' for a home, (Just a-look-in' for a home,)

Just a-look-in' for a home. (Just a-look-in' for a home.)

50

2. The first time I saw the boll weevil,
   He was sittin' on the square;
   The next time I saw the boll weevil,
   He had all of his family there,
   Just a-lookin' for a home, (Just a-lookin' for a home,)
   Just a-lookin' for a home. (Just a-lookin' for a home.)
3. The farmer took the boll weevil
   And buried him in hot sand;
   The boll weevil said to the farmer,
   "I'll stand it like a man,
   For it is my home, (For it is my home,)
   For it is my home." (For it is my home.")
4. The farmer took the boll weevil,
   And put him in a lump of ice;
   The boll weevil said to the farmer,
   "This is mighty cool and nice,
   It'll be my home, (It'll be my home,)
   It'll be my home." (It'll be my home.")
5. The boll weevil said to the farmer,
   "You better leave me alone;
   I ate up all your cotton,
   Now I'm gonna start on your corn,
   I'll have a home, (I'll have a home,)
   I'll have a home." (I'll have a home.")

PICK A BALE O' COTTON

Southern Work Song

1. Gon-na jump down, turn a-round, pick a bale o' cot-ton, Gon-na jump down, turn a-round, pick a bale a day.

(Chorus) Oh, Law-dy, pick a bale o' cot-ton, Oh, Law-dy, pick a bale a day.

2. Me and my partner can pick a bale o' cotton,
   Me and my partner can pick a bale a day.
       Chorus
3. I b'lieve to my soul I can pick a bale o' cotton,
   I b'lieve to my soul I can pick a bale a day.
       Chorus
4. Gonna pick a, pick a, pick a, pick a, pick a bale o'cotton,
   Gonna pick a, pick a, pick a, pick a, pick a bale a day.
       Chorus

* Optional chords for guitar: Key of E (E, A, B⁷)

Although impossible to hand-pick a bale (500 lbs.) of cotton in one day, this rhythmic work song livened up the workers as they bent between the thorny rows of cotton plants.

COTTON NEEDS PICKIN'

Southern Work Song

Cot-ton needs a-pick-in' so bad, Cot-ton needs a-pick-in' so bad,— Cot-ton needs a-pick-in' so bad, I'm gon-na pick all o-ver this field.

Suggestion: One group can sing "Cotton Needs Pickin' " while another group sings (at the same time) "Pick a Bale o' Cotton."

SHUCKIN' OF THE CORN

Midwest Folk Song

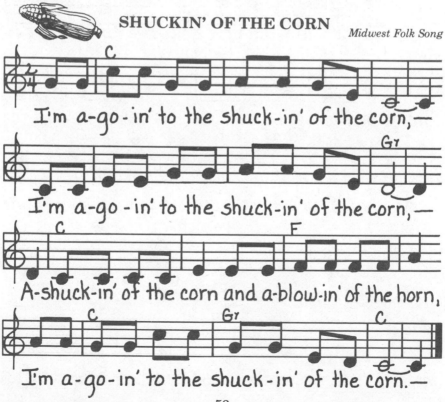

I'm a-go-in' to the shuck-in' of the corn,—
I'm a-go-in' to the shuck-in' of the corn,—
A-shuck-in' of the corn and a-blow-in' of the horn,
I'm a-go-in' to the shuck-in' of the corn.—

The Gold Rush kept prospectors following new leads across the West, but most of the searches ended in dismal failure. However, those that gave up mining often settled in the West and new communities were formed.

OLD SETTLER'S SONG

Northwest Ballad

1. I've wan-dered all o-ver this coun-try,— Pros-pect-ing and dig-ging for gold, I've tun-neled, hy-drau-licked and cra-dled, And I have been fre-quent-ly sold. And I have been fre-quent-ly sold,— And I have been fre-quent-ly sold. I've tun-neled, hy-drau-licked and cra-dled, And I have been fre-quent-ly sold.

2. For each man who got rich by mining,
   Perceiving that hundreds grew poor,
   I made up my mind to try farming,
   The only pursuit that was sure.

   Chorus: The only pursuit that was sure,
           The only pursuit that was sure,
           I made up my mind to try farming,
           The only pursuit that was sure.*

3. So, rolling my grub in my blanket,
   I left all my tools on the ground,
   I started one morning to shank it
   For the country they call Puget Sound.
           Chorus

4. When I looked on the prospects so gloomy,
   The tears trickled over my face,
   And I thought that my troubles had brought me,
   To the end of the jumping-off place.
           Chorus

5. I tried to get out of the country,
   But poverty forced me to stay,
   Until I became an old settler,
   Then nothing could drive me away.
           Chorus

6. No longer the slave of ambition,
   I laugh at the world and its shams,
   As I think of my pleasant condition
   Surrounded by acres of clams.
           Chorus

* The choruses of the remaining verses are similarly formed by repetition of the fourth and third lines.

55

During the California Gold Rush of 1849, many songs were created by putting new words to familiar tunes. This melody is Stephen Foster's "Camptown Races."

SACRAMENTO

Sea Chantey*, 1850

1. A bul-ly ship and a bul-ly crew, With a hoo-da and a hoo-da, A bul-ly mate and a cap-tain, too, Hoo-da, hoo-da ay.

(Chorus) Then blow ye winds, hi-oh, For Cal-i-for-ny-o, There's plen-ty of gold, so I've been told, On the banks of the Sac-ra-men-to.

2. Around Cape Horn in the month of snow,
   With a hoo-da, and a hoo-da,
   We came to the land where the riches flow,
   Hoo-da, hoo-da ay.
         Chorus

Suggestion: One person sings solo on first phrases, group joins in on "hoo-da's" and chorus.

---

* *A chantey (shan' ti) is a song that sailors sing in rhythm with motions while working.*

56

BLOW YE WINDS

Sea Chantey

1. 'Tis ad-ver-tised in Bos-ton town, New York and Buf-fa-lo,
Five hun-dred brave A-mer-i-cans, A-whal-ing for to go,—

Chorus
sing-ing, Blow ye winds of morn—ing; Blow ye winds, heigh-ho!
Haul a-way your run-ning gear And blow, ye winds, heigh-ho!

2. They send you to New Bedford fair,
   That famous whaling port,
   And give you to some strangers there
     To board and fit you out, singing,
       Chorus

3. They tell you of the clipper ships,
   A-running in and out,
   And say you'll take five hundred whale
     Before you're six months out, singing,
       Chorus

4. And now we're out to sea, my boys,
   The wind comes on to blow,
   One half the watch is sick on deck,
     The other half below, singing,
       Chorus

*Optional chords for guitar: Key of E (E, B⁷, A, F#⁷)

During the 1760's, colonists in New Bedford, Massachusetts began a whaling industry. The greatest period of American whaling was from 1830-60. When a whaling ship left port, the crew could expect a two-year voyage filled with thrills and danger.

CAPE COD CHANTEY

Sea Chantey

1. Cape Cod girls, they have no combs, Heave a-way, heave a-way, They comb their hair with cod-fish bones, We are bound for Aus-tra-lia!

Chorus Heave a-way, ye bul-ly, bul-ly boys, Heave a-way, heave a-way, Heave a-way and don't ye make a noise, We are bound for Aus-tra-lia.

2. Cape Cod boys, they have no sleds, heave away, heave away,
   They slide downhill on codfish heads, we are bound for Australia.
   Chorus
3. Cape Cod men, they have no sails, heave away, heave away,
   They sail their boats with codfish tails, we are bound for Australia.
   Chorus
4. Cape Cod wives, they have no pins, heave away, heave away,
   They pin their gowns with codfish fins, we are bound for Australia.
   Chorus

The Black Ball Line were ships that carried mail and freight between Liverpool and New York beginning in 1818. Each ship carried a crimson swallow-tail flag with a black ball in the center.

BLOW THE MAN DOWN

Sea Chantey

1. Come-all you young fel-lows that fol-low the sea, With a way, hey, blow the man down, Now please, pay at-ten-tion and lis-ten to me, Give me some time to blow the man down.

2. There are tinkers and tailors, shoemakers and all,
   With a way, hey, blow the man down,
   They're all shipped for sailors on board the Black Ball,
   Give me some time to blow the man down.
3. 'Tis when the Black Baller is clear of the land,
   With a way, hey, blow the man down,
   The crew musters aft at the word of command,
   Give me some time to blow the man down.
4. Pay attention to orders, now you, one and all,
   With a way, hey, blow the man down,
   For see, right above you there flies the Black Ball,
   Give me some time to blow the man down.

The Erie Canal, completed in 1825 between Buffalo and Albany, New York, joined the Great Lakes System with the Atlantic Ocean. Boats were pulled by mules which walked alongside the canal on towpaths. The muledrivers were called towpath boys or "hoggies."

ERIE CANAL

Canal Work Song

1. I've got a mule, her name is Sal, Fif-teen

miles on the E-rie Ca-nal. She's a good old

work-er and a good old pal. Fif-teen

miles on the E-rie Ca-nal. We've hauled some

bar-ges in our day, Filled with lum-ber,

coal and hay, And we know ev-'ry inch of the

way, From Al-ba-ny to — Buf—fa-lo.—

Chorus

Low bridge, ev'-ry-bod-y down, Low bridge, for we're

com-in' to a town; And you'll al-ways know your

neigh-bor, You'll al-ways know your pal, If you've

ev-er nav-i-gat-ed on the E-rie Ca-nal.

2. Git up there, Sal, we passed that lock,
   Fifteen miles on the Erie Canal,
And we'll make Rome 'fore six o'clock,
   Fifteen miles on the Erie Canal.
Just one more trip and back we'll go
   Through the rain and sleet and snow,
'Cause we know ev'ry inch of the way
   From Albany to Buffalo.
      Chorus

61

DOWN THE RIVER

River Chantey

1. The riv-er is up and the chan-nel is deep,

The wind is stead-y and strong,— Oh, won't we

have a jol-ly good time As we go sail-ing a-long.

Chorus

Down the riv-er, oh, down the riv-er, Oh,

down the riv-er we go,—— Down the riv-er, oh,

down the riv-er, Oh, down the O-hi-o.——

2. The river is up and the channel is deep, the wind is steady and strong,
   Oh, Dinah, put the hoecake on, as we go sailing along.
   Chorus
3. The river is up and the channel is deep, the wind is steady and strong,
   The waves do splash from shore to shore, as we go sailing along.
   Chorus

INDEX